TEN IN A BED

Mary Rees

Joy Street Books

Little, Brown and Company

BOSTON · TORONTO

First U.S. Edition

Library of Congress Catalog Card Number 87-82848

10   9   8   7   6   5   4   3   2

Joy Street Books are published by Little, Brown and Company (Inc.)
Printed in England

There were TEN in the bed

And the little one said,
"Roll over! Roll over!"
So they all rolled over
And one fell out . . .

There were NINE in the bed
And the little one said,
"Roll over! Roll over!"
So they all rolled over
And one fell out . . .

There were EIGHT in the bed
And the little one said,
"Roll over! Roll over!"
So they all rolled over
And one fell out . . .

There were SEVEN in the bed
And the little one said,
"Roll over! Roll over!"
So they all rolled over
And one fell out . . .

There were SIX in the bed
And the little one said,
"Roll over! Roll over!"
So they all rolled over
And one fell out . . .

There were FIVE in the bed
And the little one said,
"Roll over! Roll over!"
So they all rolled over
And one fell out . . .

There were FOUR in the bed
And the little one said,
"Roll over! Roll over!"
So they all rolled over
And one fell out . . .

There were THREE in the bed
And the little one said,
"Roll over! Roll over!"
So they all rolled over
And one fell out . . .

There were TWO in the bed
And the little one said,
"Roll over! Roll over!"
So they all rolled over
And one fell out . . .

There was ONE in the bed
And the little one said,
"I'm not getting up!"
The other NINE said,
"Oh, yes, you are!"

Then there were NONE in the bed
And no one said,
"Roll over! Roll over!"